W9-APX-771

E
MAC

MacDonald, Amy.

Rachel Fister's
blister.

$14.25

Preschool
04-1203

DATE			

Rachel Fister's Blister

Amy MacDonald

Illustrations by Marjorie Priceman

Houghton Mifflin Company   Boston

For Emily — A.M.

For Elizabeth — M.P.

Library of Congress Cataloging-in-Publication Data

MacDonald, Amy.
   Rachel Fister's blister/Amy MacDonald; illustrations by
Marjorie Priceman.
      p. cm.
   Summary: Rachel Fister's blister sends adults scurrying for a
cure, but nothing seems to help until they appeal to the Queen for
advice.
   RNF ISBN 0-395-52152-1   PA ISBN 0-395-65744-X
   [1. Wounds and injuries—Fiction. 2. Stories in rhyme.]
I. Priceman, Marjorie, ill. II. Title.
PZ8.3.M146Rac   1990   90-4388
[E]—dc20   CIP
                             AC

Printed in the United States of America

WOZ   20 19 18 17 16

Rachel Fister
found a blister
on her little left-hand toe.

Just a tiny
little blister,
but she thought her mom should know.

Mrs. Fister
saw the blister
on poor Rachel's little toe,

Sent for Mister
(Harvey) Fister,
for she thought he ought to know.

"Don't alarm her.
Bring the farmer!
Call the doctor, call the nurse!

"We need help to
fix the blister —
Now — before it gets much worse!

"Find her brothers
and some others.
Send them off to bring some aid.

"Go enlist her
little sister.
Fetch the rabbi. Fetch the maid.

"Quicker! Faster!
Bring the pastor!
Call the postman! Call the priest!

"Faster! Quicker!
Bring the vicar!
Call the fireman! Call the p'lice!

"They'll assist her
with the blister.
Yes, I think they ought to know

"How to fix a
little blister
like the one on Rachel's toe."

13

Pastor Masters
called for plasters —
six or eight or ten or three.

Farmer Chalmer
was much calmer —
he suggested broccoli.

15

Doctor Proctor
said, "Concoct her
up an herbal remedy,"

While the p'liceman
and the postman
both advised a cup of tea.

Rachel's brothers
(and some others)
swore that *ice* would do the trick;

But the fireman
(Roger Byreman)
said that *heat* would cure it quick.

Vicar Wicker
called for liquor
(what he meant was lemonade),

While the maids and
ladies bickered
and the priest and rabbi prayed.

21

Well, they tried them —
they applied them —
one by one to Rachel's toe.

22

"Darling daughter,
is that better?"
But each time she answered, "No."

"This is irksome.
This is quirksome.
Surely someone ought to know.

"Surely someone
can assist her
with the blister on her toe?"

"Call the palace.
Ask Queen Alice.
She's the smartest,
that's for sure."

25

So they called her
and appalled her
with their tale of Rachel's cure.

"Fire and ice and tea and spice!" exclaimed the Queen. "Such silly tips!

"My advice is quite precise: it's — listen up! —

Just *use your lips*."

"O clever Queen!
(What *can* she mean?)"
Asked the rabbi and the priest.

And the others —
doctors, brothers —
all were stumped, to say the least.

Rachel's mother
said, "Don't bother,
for I think that I can guess."

And she *kissed* her
daughter's blister.
"Is that better, daughter?"

"YES!"